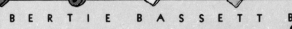

BERTIE BASSETT B

CW00846967

Bertie's
MAGIC GARDEN

by
Wendy Hobson

illustrated by
Carla Shale

Ω Quiller Press

One sunny, spring day, Lucy and Simon were on their way to school. Bertie was standing at his front door.

"It's a perfect day for gardening," said Bertie. "And I could do with some help."

"As long as I can do the digging," called Lucy. "See you later."

After breakfast, Bertie went into the garden. What a mess! The lawn and the path were quite overgrown and the flower beds were full of weeds.

Bertie worked hard all day, digging, weeding, planting and trimming. Allsorts loved nuzzling into the piles of weeds. He tossed them in the air. Then he turned and brushed them back into piles with his tail before Bertie could tell him off for making a mess. Looking out of the corner of his eye, Bertie could see exactly what Allsorts was doing. But he pretended not to notice.

By the time the children came home from school, Bertie had the garden looking much tidier. And with three pairs of hands — and two pairs of paws — planting the flowers and seeds took no time at all.

8

"Now for the vegetables," said Bertie, putting down a box of sprouting potatoes next to the vegetable patch.

"They are just old potatoes," said Lucy.

"Yes," replied Bertie. "But there is magic in a garden that makes old things grow into new ones."

It was raining the next day. The gardeners read Bertie's gardening books and looked through the packets of seeds which he had collected from all over the world.

"My favourite is the Chilly fire bush," said Lucy as she looked at the pictures. Puzzled, Bertie looked at the packet which she held out to him.

"You mean 'Chilean '", he laughed. "That's where it comes from." He brought down his globe from a top shelf, and showed them a long, thin country round the other side of the world.

"Is it always cold there?" asked Lucy.

"No," said Bertie. "It just sounds as though it should be."

They were now very keen on gardening. Their father could not understand it because they had never wanted to help him before. But he made them their own flower beds in the garden.

At school, they painted egg shells to look like people. Then they sprinkled tiny seeds on some cotton wool inside. Lucy proudly showed her mother the beautiful crop of hair on her space

monster's head. But Simon had pushed his red indian into the bottom of his bag. When he brought it out, Mrs Green could see why. It was nothing but a few wispy shoots.

"I've got brown fingers," grumbled Simon. "I can't grow anything. Even the seeds in my garden look as though they would rather be somewhere else."

Bertie knew just how to cheer him up. He had some glass cold frames in his garden, and he covered one with black plastic. The children noticed it at once and tried to see what was underneath.

"It must be something special," said Lucy. "Could it be a lovely flower which only blooms once in a hundred years?"

"Or a seed that grows into the tallest flower in the world," said Simon.

When Bertie came out, they asked him what it was.

"Oh, that's just my magic garden," he said.

The children were bursting to know all about it. But they groaned as their mum called them in for tea.

"Trust Mrs Green to be on time with the tea, Allsorts," said Bertie, "otherwise our magic would have gone up in smoke!" Bertie just had time to search round the house and slip two small things under the plastic before the children rushed back.

"Tell us how you made the earth magic," said Lucy excitedly.

"Certainly not," frowned Bertie, trying to look serious. "You have to treat the magic garden carefully, because it only works once. Kneel down and think about something you would really like at this moment."

As they knelt down, Bertie thought his plans were ruined. For there was Allsorts digging in the earth with the torn plastic flapping over his head. As the naughty dog came out, Bertie smiled with relief.

"It works!" cried the children. For between Allsorts' teeth he held a large juicy bone.

"Quickly", said Bertie, "before the magic disappears. Put your hand under the cover, Lucy."

She stretched out her hand and felt under the plastic.

"There's a soft thing," she said, "and something papery and flat. How do I know which is the one I wished for?"

"No one else does," laughed Bertie. "You must choose."

So Lucy drew out her hand. She was holding a tiny, red, silken flower.

"It's lovely," she said. "And it's even better than a real flower because it will last a hundred years!"

Simon pushed his hand under the plastic and drew out a small envelope with the words: GOOD RESULTS EVERY TIME on the back. Inside was a handful of seeds.

"Are they sure to grow?" asked Simon. "Most things I plant don't grow right at all."

"Even the best gardeners can't grow everything," Bertie comforted him. "But they are magic seeds, and I am sure they will grow."

Simon smiled. He would show everyone that he could grow something extra special.

For the next few weeks, the children worked in the garden now and then. To his delight, Simon's seedlings were soon larger than Lucy's. It was not long before he needed stakes as tall as his father to keep them upright. Then he watched with pride as the buds formed on the top and flowered into a row of beautiful sunflowers.

Simon was very pleased with his flowers. He thought about Bertie's garden magic turning old things into new ones. And he wondered if a little of the magic might have rubbed off on his fingers.

It would soon be his birthday, and he very much wanted some new cars. What if he could surprise everyone by making his old cars look like new! He found a box of his old cars, some paint and brushes. When everyone else was busy, he went into the shed and tried to give them a new coat of paint.

But the magic did not work! There was more paint on his fingers than on the cars. And they did not look new at all, just a bit of a mess. He decided to give up.

Bertie had seen him working in the shed, and how unhappy he looked when he came out again. He decided to find out what Simon was up to. That evening, he and Mr Green went down to the shed with a torch, and found the half-painted cars hidden in their box.

"So that's it," said Bertie. "New potatoes for old, new cars for old!" He took the cars home, leaving the box in the shed so Simon would not miss them.

After that, Simon and Lucy noticed that Bertie was acting rather strangely. One day, Allsorts made them wait on the step until Bertie called, "You can come in now."

They could see that Bertie had quickly pushed something into a kitchen cupboard because there was a corner of newspaper poking out of the door. Then Bertie tried to wipe some spots of paint off Allsorts' paws without being noticed.

"We came to ask you both to my birthday party on Saturday," said Simon.

"We'll look forward to it," said Bertie. "And I just hope we are ready in time," he added in a whisper to Allsorts, as he watched the children walk back down the path.

The party was a great success. There were games, music and dancing. The table was loaded with green and yellow jellies, iced biscuits and crisps. In the middle, was a wonderful birthday cake in shape of a sunflower. When Bertie arrived, he sent Allsorts into the room and peered round the door.

"I found something belonging to you," he said to Simon. He staggered in holding a large plant in a pot. Hanging from the stems were Simon's old cars; but they did not look old any more. Every one had a new coat of paint which shone as they twizzled round on their cotton threads.

"So the magic works after all!" laughed Simon "Thank you, Bertie."

"If you wish for something hard enough," smiled Bertie, "and work for it, too, then sometimes it can have a funny way of coming true."